Plateosaurus
The selfish dinosaur

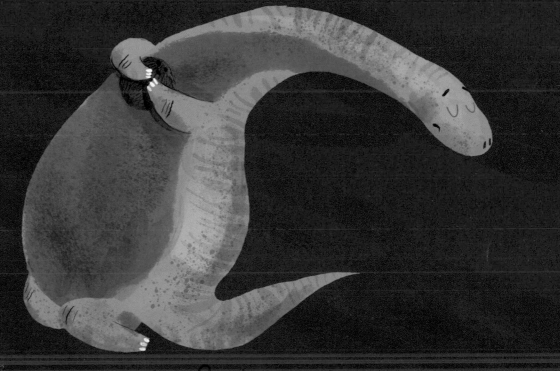

Written by Catherine Veitch

Illustrated by Catalina Echeverri

MILES KELLY

A young Plateosaurus called Posy once lived near a **dusty desert**. She had the best spot beside a river.

Posy was a **selfish** dinosaur. If she found her favourite liverwort leaves growing nearby, she wouldn't tell her friends.

"There's no liverwort here," she would say, and send them looking in the **opposite direction**.

Every day, Posy played rock skittles. There was always a queue of other dinosaurs waiting to play.

But Posy wouldn't share.

Once, a brave little Eoraptor called Esme dared to ask for a turn in her BIGGEST voice.

"Please can I play?"

Posy held on tight to her rock and said, "No, you can't play! These are MY skittles! Go away!"

Each day, dinosaurs had to **cross a bridge** over the river to reach the shady trees on the other side.

Posy wouldn't let them cross.
She said, "This is MY bridge
and you can't cross here."
So all the dinosaurs had to
go the longer way round.

WAAAHH!

Things carried on like this until a new dinosaur moved into the desert.

His name was Malik and he was a Melanorosaurus. And Malik was just as selfish as Posy.

One hot day, Malik started
to cross the bridge to
reach the shady side
of the river.

"Get off MY bridge!" shouted Posy.
"It's MY bridge now!" shouted Malik.

The other dinosaurs suggested that Posy and Malik have a competition.

The winner of the competition would be the owner of the bridge. First they had a race.

Next there was a log-lifting contest to see who was the strongest. Posy gripped a log in her jaws and heaved it in the air.

But Malik hauled an even bigger log higher than Posy did. "Malik is the winner!" shouted Charlie the Coelophysis.

"Who can jump the highest?" asked Esme. Posy and Malik both leapt into the air at the same time.

Esme and Charlie measured their jumps.

"I won, I won!" shouted Posy. "No you didn't! I jumped higher than you!" shouted Malik.

There was a hush as the winner was announced...

"It's... a draw!" said Charlie.

Posy and Malik had both won. They were too **surprised** to speak!

But Posy and Malik didn't like being winners together. They didn't want to share the bridge.

Then from the forest came a
huge, stomping, roaring beast.

It marched towards the bridge.

"It's a Euskelosaurus! RUUUN!" shouted Posy and Malik to the little dinosaurs.

RAAA!

There was a crazy bundle as the little dinosaurs sped off.

Posy and Malik stood side-by-side on the bridge. "No one is crossing OUR bridge!" they said.

They rose onto their back legs and bared their teeth and claws. "RAAA!" they snarled.

Posy and Malik's plan worked! The Euskelosaurus turned its back and **slunk away** into the forest.

"He won't dare step on OUR bridge again!" they laughed.

Everyone heard how Posy and Malik worked together to scare away the Euskelosaurus.

"Has the **mean dinosaur** really gone?" asked Esme. "Yes, and it's not coming back," smiled Posy.

"It's more fun doing things together," Posy said. Malik agreed, and from then on they **shared** the bridge with everyone.